LOVE
SELECTED POEMS

by **e. e. cummings**

art by **christopher myers**

jump at the sun
hyperion books for children

we love each other very dearly

                                         , more
than raindrops need sunbeams or snowflakes make
possible mayflowers:

                              quite eyes of air
not with twilight's first thrushes may awake
more secretly than our(if disappear
should some world)selves

.No doing shall undo
(nor madness nor mere death nor both who is
la guerre)your me or simplify my you
,darling

        sweet this creative never known
complexity was born before the moon
before God wished Himself into a rose

and even(
              we'll adventure the into
most immemorial of whens
)before

each heartbeat which i am alive to kiss

since feeling is first
who pays any attention
to the syntax of things
will never wholly kiss you;

wholly to be a fool
while Spring is in the world

my blood approves,

and kisses are a better fate
than wisdom
lady i swear by all flowers. Don't cry
—the best gesture of my brain is less than
your eyelids' flutter which says

we are for each other: then
laugh, leaning back in my arms
for life's not a paragraph

And death i think is no parenthesis

in the rain-
darkness,   the sunset
being sheathed i sit and
think of you

the holy
city which is your face
your little cheeks the streets
of smiles

your eyes half-
thrush
half-angel and your drowsy
lips where float flowers of kiss

and
there is the sweet shy pirouette
your hair
and then

your dancesong
soul. rarely-beloved
a single star is
uttered, and i

think
        of you

up into the silence the green
silence with a white earth in it

you will(kiss me)go

out into the morning the young
morning with a warm world in it

(kiss me)you will go

on into the sunlight the fine
sunlight with a firm day in it

you will go(kiss me

down into your memory and
a memory and memory

i)kiss me(will go)

love is more thicker than forget
more thinner than recall
more seldom than a wave is wet
more frequent than to fail

it is most mad and moonly
and less it shall unbe
than all the sea which only
is deeper than the sea

love is less always than to win
less never than alive
less bigger than the least begin
less littler than forgive

it is most sane and sunly
and more it cannot die
than all the sky which only
is higher than the sky

trees
      were in(give
give)bud when to me
you
made for by love
love said did
o no yes

earth was in
                (live
live)spring
with all beautiful
things when to
me
you gave gave darling

birds are
         in(trees are in)
song
when to me you
leap and i'm born we
're sunlight of
oneness

open your heart:
i'll give you a treasure
of tiniest world
a piece of forever with

summitless younger than
angels are mountains
rivery forests
towerful towns(queen

poet king float
sprout heroes of moonstar
flutter to and
swim blossoms of person)through

musical shadows while hunted
by daemons
seethe luminous
leopards(on wingfeet of thingfear)

come ships go
snowily sailing
perfect silence.
Absolute ocean

may my heart always be open to little
birds who are the secrets of living
whatever they sing is better than to know
and if men should not hear them men are old

may my mind stroll about hungry
and fearless and thirsty and supple
and even if it's sunday may i be wrong
for whenever men are right they are not young

and may myself do nothing usefully
and love yourself so more than truly
there's never been quite such a fool who could fail
pulling all the sky over him with one smile

move
deeply,rain
(dream hugely)wish
firmly.   splendidly advancing colour

strike
into form
(actually)realness
kill

(make
strangely)known(establish
new)come,what
Being!open us open

our
selves. create
(suddenly announce:hurl)
blind full steep love

may i feel said he
(i'll squeal said she
just once said he)
it's fun said she

(may i touch said he
how much said she
a lot said he)
why not said she

(let's go said he
not too far said she
what's too far said he
where you are said she)

may i stay said he
(which way said she
like this said he
if you kiss said she

may i move said he
is it love said she)
if you're willing said he
(but you're killing said she

but it's life said he
but your wife said she
now said he)
ow said she

(tiptop said he
don't stop said she
oh no said he)
go slow said she

(cccome?said he
ummm said she)
you're divine!said he
(you are Mine said she)

the moon looked into my window
it touched me with its small hands
and with curling infantile
fingers it understood my eyes cheeks mouth
its hands(slipping)felt of my necktie wandered
against my shirt and into my body the
sharp things fingered tinily my heart life

the little hands withdrew, jerkily, themselves

quietly they began playing with a button
the moon smiled she
let go my vest and crept
through the window
she did not fall
she went creeping along the air

                                    over houses
                                            roofs

And out of the east toward
her a fragile light bent gatheringly

when my love comes to see me it's
just a little like music,a
little more like curving colour (say
orange)
                against silence, or darkness . . . .

the coming of my love emits
a wonderful smell in my mind,

you should see when i turn to find
her how my least heart-beat becomes less.
And then all her beauty is a vise

whose stilling lips murder suddenly me,

but of my corpse the tool her smile makes something
suddenly luminous and precise

—and then we are I and She . . . .

what is that the hurdy-gurdy's playing

the moon is hiding in
her hair.
The
lily
of heaven
full of all dreams,
draws down.

cover her briefness in singing
close her with intricate faint birds
by daisies and twilights
Deepen her,

Recite
upon her
flesh
the rain's

pearls singly-whispering.

All in green went my love riding
on a great horse of gold
into the silver dawn.

four lean hounds crouched low and smiling
the merry deer ran before.

Fleeter be they than dappled dreams
the swift sweet deer
the red rare deer.

Four red roebuck at a white water
the cruel bugle sang before.

Horn at hip went my love riding
riding the echo down
into the silver dawn. . . .

is there a flower(whom
i meet anywhere
able to be and seem
so quite softly as your hair

what bird has perfect fear
(of suddenly me)like these
first deepest rare
quite who are your eyes

(shall any dream
come a more millionth mile
shyly to its doom
than you will smile)

love our so right
is,all(each thing
most lovely)sweet
things cannot spring
but we be they'll

some or if where
shall breathe a new
(silverly rare
goldenly so)
moon,she is you

nothing may,quite
your my(my your
and)self without,
completely dare
be beautiful

one if should sing
(at yes of day)
younger than young
bird first for joy,
he's i he's i

it is so long since my heart has been with yours

shut by our mingling arms through
a darkness where new lights begin and
increase,
since your mind has walked into
my kiss as a stranger
into the streets and colours of a town—

that I have perhaps forgotten
how, always(from
these hurrying crudities
of blood and flesh)Love
coins His most gradual gesture,

and whittles life to eternity

—after which our separating selves become museums
filled with skilfully stuffed memories

somewhere i have never travelled,gladly beyond
any experience,your eyes have their silence:
in your most frail gesture are things which enclose me,
or which i cannot touch because they are too near

your slightest look easily will unclose me
though i have closed myself as fingers,
you open always petal by petal myself as Spring opens
(touching, skilfully,mysteriously)her first rose

or if your wish be to close me,i and
my life will shut very beautifully,suddenly,
as when the heart of this flower imagines
the snow carefully everywhere descending;

nothing which we are to perceive in this world equals
the power of your intense fragility:whose texture
compels me with the colour of its countries,
rendering death and forever with each breathing

(i do not know what it is about you that closes
and opens;only something in me understands
the voice of your eyes is deeper than all roses)
nobody,not even the rain,has such small hands

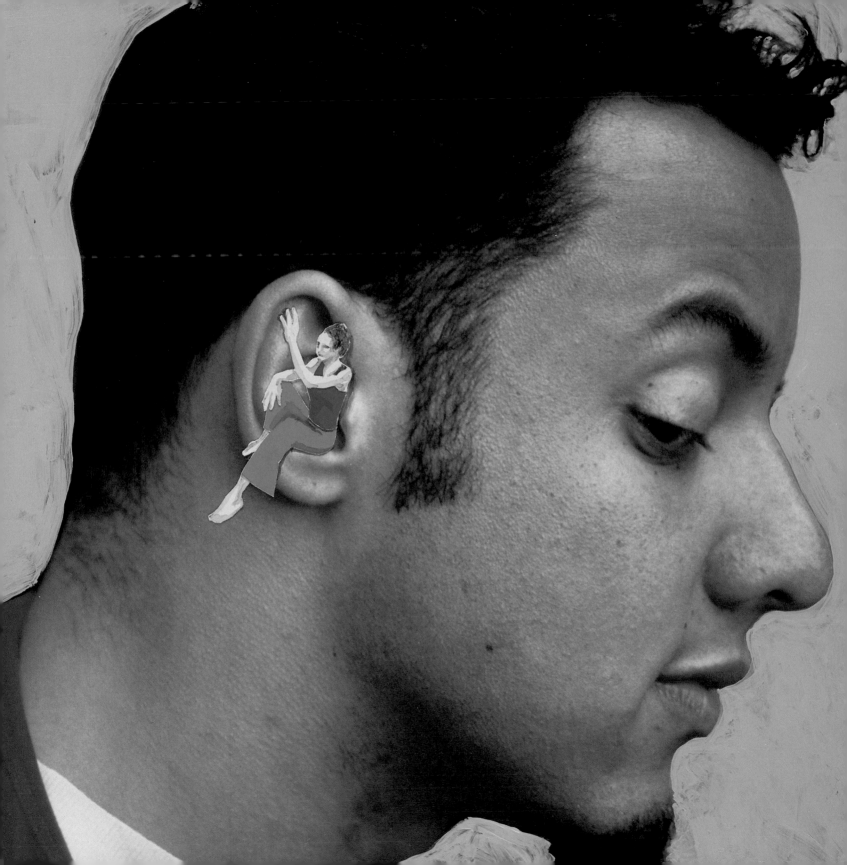

(once like a spark)

if strangers meet
life begins—
not poor not rich
(only aware)
kind neither
nor cruel
(only complete)
i not not you
not possible;
only truthful
—truthfully,once
if strangers(who
deep our most are
selves)touch:
forever

(and so to dark)

Special thanks to:
Azza Satti, Leyla Mei, Alexis Agathacleous,
Ismail Lawal, Sagal Abshir, Hisham Bharoocha,
Greg Clark, Tunde Oyewole, Alberto Rivera,
Micheline Brown, Dega Abshir, Shin Ishizuka,
Natalie Burnham, Olivia Mori, Ryna Villar,
Rachel Boynton, Mike Crawford, Kiki Thorpe,
Naeem Mohaiemen, Rekha Viswanathan,
Stephen Sprott, and especially
Erin Shigaki for her wonderful design skills.